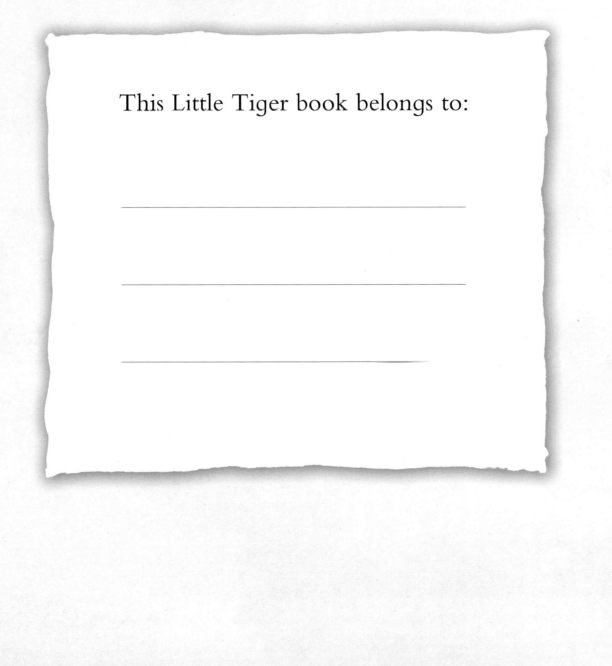

This Little Tiger book belongs to:

_____

_____

_____

For Georgie and Olivia

T W

Dotty was very excited.
It was her birthday, and she
had lots of cards to open.

But where were all Dotty's friends?

Dotty went to find Pip the mouse.
Instead she found a little round
present with her name on it!

What could it be?

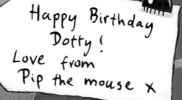

Happy Birthday
Dotty!
Love from
Pip the mouse x

Hooray!

A bouncy ball!

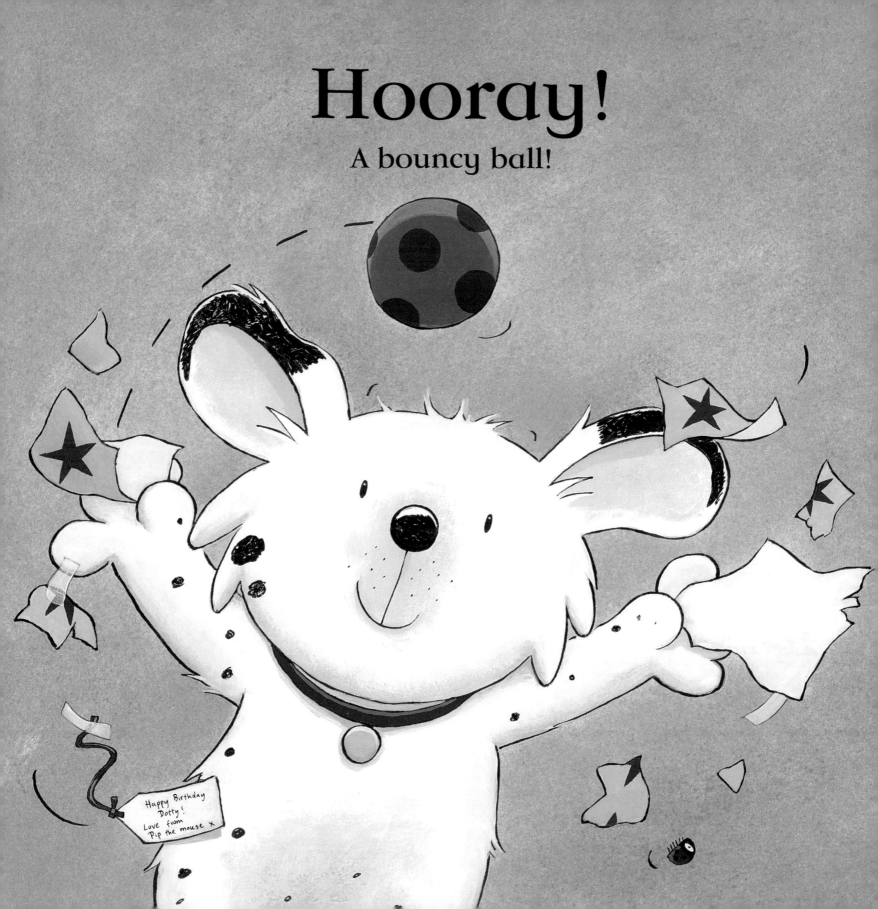

Happy Birthday
Dotty!
Love from
Pip the mouse x

As she chased after it,
Dotty spotted an arrow
on the floor. It pointed
to another and another.

It was a birthday trail!

Dotty followed the arrows . . .

. . . to the sandpit, where there was *another* parcel. Dotty read the label. "Happy Birthday, Dotty, love from Tommy the tortoise."

What was it?

Delicious!

A yummy bone!

Dotty hurried across the garden, following the arrows to . . .

. . . Susie's apple tree. Leaning against her nest was another present!

Yippee!

It was a kite from Susie!

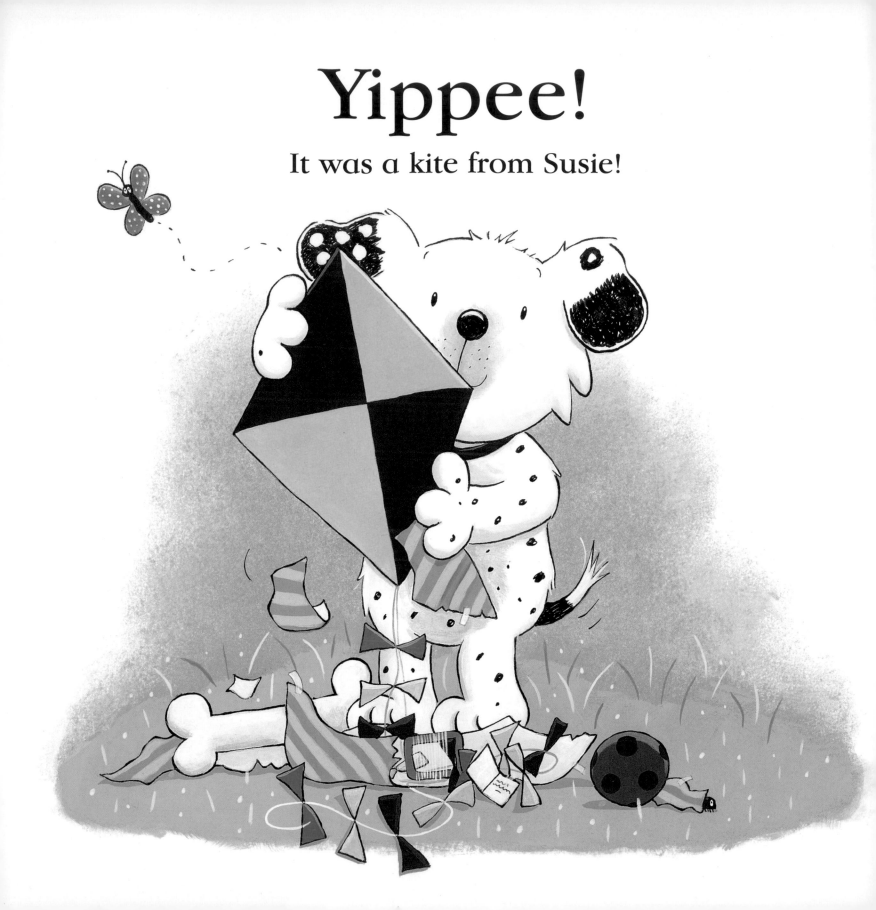

But Susie wasn't there to help fly it.
Where was everyone?

Dotty was puzzled.
Taking all her presents,
she skipped along the trail
of arrows to . . .

. . .Whiskers the rabbit's hutch.
Dotty saw another funny-shaped present.
She read, "Happy Birthday, Dotty,
love from Whiskers."

Dotty began to
unwrap it . . .

Wow!

A trike!

Dotty squealed with delight.
She popped all her
presents into the trailer.
She'd had lots of surprises,
but still Dotty's friends
were nowhere to
be seen.

Where could they be?
Maybe they had followed
the arrows too. Dotty
climbed on to her
shiny new trike and . . .

WHEEE!

She went to look for her friends.

Suddenly the trail ended.

Dotty was amazed to find . .

. . . the
BIGGEST PRESENT
she had ever seen!

Dotty danced round
and round in circles.
What could this be?

"SURPRISE!
HAPPY BIRTHDAY, DOTTY!"

LITTLE TIGER PRESS LTD,
an imprint of the Little Tiger Group
1 Coda Studios, 189 Munster Road,
London SW6 6AW
www.littletiger.co.uk

First published in Great Britain 2003
This edition published 2020
Text copyright © Tim Warnes 2003
Illustrations copyright © Tim Warnes 2003
www.timwarnes.com

Tim Warnes has asserted his rights to be
identified as the author and illustrator of this
work under the Copyright, Designs and
Patents Act, 1988

All rights reserved • ISBN 978-1-78881-806-3
Printed in China • LTP/1800/3245/0320
2 4 6 8 10 9 7 5 3 1